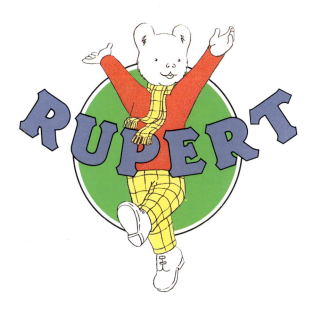

MEET ALL THESE FRIENDS IN BUZZ BOOKS:

Thomas the Tank Engine
The Animals of Farthing Wood
Biker Mice From Mars
James Bond Junior
Fireman Sam
Joshua Jones
Rupert
Babar

First published in Great Britain 1994 by Buzz Books,
an imprint of Reed Children's Books
Michelin House, 81 Fulham Road, London, SW3 6RB
and Auckland, Melbourne, Singapore and Toronto

ISBN 1 8559 382 8

Printed in Italy by Olivotto

RUPERT™

and the

MAGIC SHELL

Story by Norman Redfern
Illustrations by SPJ Design

It was the first day of Rupert's holiday in Rocky Bay. He ran down to the sea.

"Ahoy there!" said a cheerful voice.

Rupert waved to Captain Binnacle.

It was peaceful in the little harbour. Rupert bent down to look at the wet pebbles as they sparkled in the sunshine.

Suddenly, a big wave roared over the stones. Rupert jumped. The water bubbled around his toes, then rolled away, and the sea was calm once again.

Rupert looked down. The wave had left behind a beautiful seashell. He picked it up and took it back to the cottage.

"Look what I found, Mummy," he said, handing his mother the shell.

She put the shell to her ear.

"Do you know what I hear?" she asked.

Rupert shook his head.

"The sea!" said Mrs Bear.

Curious, Rupert held the shell close to his ear. From deep inside came a distant roar, like the waves in the bay.

"The sea!" he whispered.

He listened again. This time he heard something else.

"Help! Help!"

There was a faint voice calling.

"Help me!" came the voice again.

9

Rupert knew the voice at once. He
jumped up.

"The Merboy!" he cried. "He could be in
danger! I must go back to the beach!"

He put the shell in his pocket and
rushed out of the holiday cottage.

"Be careful, Rupert!" said his mother.

Down at the water's edge, Rupert put the shell to his ear again.

"Help!" said the Merboy's voice. "I can't climb off the rocks!"

Beyond the harbour was a rocky point.
Rupert ran across the beach and onto the
rocks. He looked up. There was the
Merboy sitting on a ledge in the cliffs.

"How did you get there?" asked Rupert.

"I was swimming in the bay at high tide
when suddenly, there was a very big
wave. It picked me up and carried me
up here," said the Merboy.

"I grabbed onto this rock, and the wave
swept past me into the harbour." The
Merboy looked out to sea. "Now the tide
has gone out, and I can't climb down.
Help me, Rupert, please!"

"Don't worry," said Rupert. "I'll go and get help!"

"Please hurry!" cried the Merboy.

Rupert climbed quickly back over the
rocks and ran to Captain Binnacle's cabin.

He rang the bell, but there was no
answer. He knocked on the door. Still
there was no reply.

"You'll be looking for the Captain."

A fisherman was sitting on a nearby
rock, mending his nets.

"He'll not be long," said the man. "He's
only sailing once around the bay."

Rupert set off back down the path.

"I know!" he said to himself. "I can wave to Captain Binnacle from the top of the cliffs."

Rupert looked out across the bay. In the far distance, he could just make out a long, low shape bobbing in the water.

"That doesn't look like the Captain's boat," he thought.

Then the shape turned and lifted his head. It was the Sea Serpent!

Rupert waved his arms above his head.
The Sea Serpent seemed to be looking
straight at him. He waved again, and
pointed down to the rocks where the
Merboy was trapped.

Suddenly, the Serpent nodded his head,
and began swimming towards the shore.
Rupert turned and ran back down the
path as fast as he could to where the
Merboy was waiting on the ledge.

"Rupert!" cried the Merboy. "You said you were bringing help!"

Rupert pointed out to sea.

"He's on his way!" he said.

Just then, the Sea Serpent came around the rocky point.

"Hello, Rupert," said the Serpent. "Whatever's the matter?"

"The Merboy," said Rupert. "He's stuck!"

"Don't worry, Merboy," said the Serpent. "I'll soon have you down!"

The Sea Serpent swam to the edge of the cliffs and craned his long neck upwards.

"Put your arms around my neck and hold on tight," he told the Merboy.

Then he dipped his head and lowered the Merboy into the calm sea.

"Oh, thank you, Sea Serpent!" said the Merboy.

"You must thank Rupert for fetching me," said the Sea Serpent. "But why didn't you use your magic shell to call for my help?"

"I've lost it," said the Merboy. "It was swept away by that big wave."

Rupert took the beautiful shell out of
his pocket.

"Is this it?" he asked.

"Yes!" cried the Merboy. "Where did
you find it?"

Rupert told his friends about the wave
which had roared up on the beach, and
left the shell at his feet that morning.

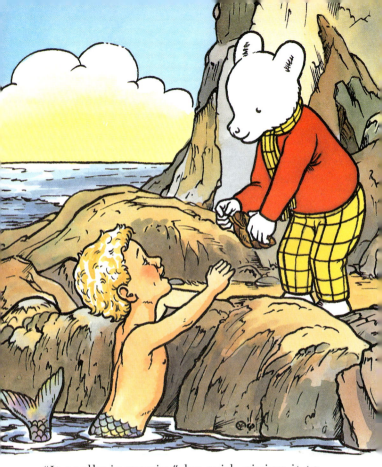

"It really is magic," he said, giving it to the Merboy. "When I held it to my ear, I could hear you calling for help."

"I'm so glad you found it," said the Merboy. "Thank you."

Rupert waved goodbye and scrambled towards the harbour. He breathed in the fresh sea air and smiled. How he loved his holidays at Rocky Bay!

"Wait, Rupert!"

It was the Merboy. He was holding the most beautiful seashell Rupert had ever seen, more beautiful even than the Merboy's magic shell.

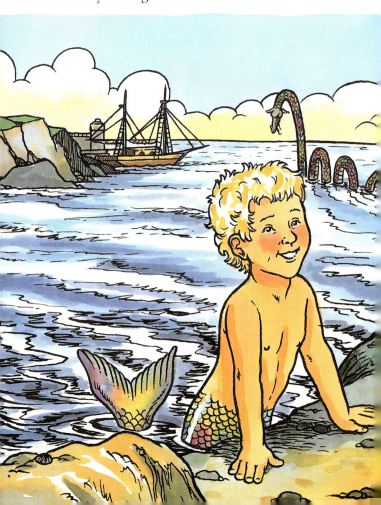

"It's for you!" said the Merboy.

Rupert took the shell home to Nutwood after his holiday. And whenever there was a cold, damp or gloomy day, he held it to his ear, and listened to the sea.

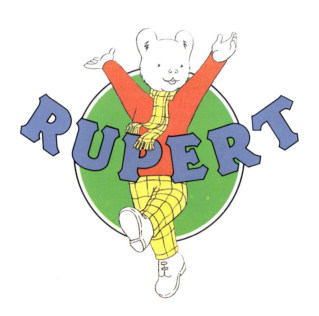